CW01668691

CLASS ACTS

STAR SCHOOL ON TOUR

Une histoire mise en scène par

Michaela Morgan

et illustrée par Cathy Brett

didier

… et encore merci à Soizic Cornet et Caroline Moreau, dont l'enthousiasme et la connaissance des élèves ont aidé cet ouvrage à trouver la bonne altitude !

Direction artistique : Mandy Norman
Maquette intérieure et composition : Becky Chilcott
Édition : Catherine Laurent, Sandrine Paniel
Enregistrements : Studio Corby

 – ISBN 978-2-278-07933-9 – ISSN 2271-7269
Dépôt légal : 7933/01 – Achevé d'imprimer en Italie en mars 2014 par Grafica Veneta

paper planes *teens*

Une collection imaginée avec humour, enthousiasme et provocation par Rupert Morgan

Tous les titres que vous pourrez enfin lire en anglais !

Débutant
A1→A2

- What is Brian? *Rupert Morgan*
- Welcome to Star School, *Michaela Morgan*
- Panic at Star School, *Michaela Morgan*
- Star School on Tour, *Michaela Morgan*

Intermédiaire
A2→B1

- Macbeth and the Creature from Hell, *Roger Morris*
- Romeo and Juliet in Las Vegas, *Rupert Morgan*
- Bubonic Britain, *Philippa Boston*
- Deadly Jobs, *Philippa Boston*
- Blitz Britain, *Philippa Boston*
- Killer Sports, *Philippa Boston*

Avancé
B1→B2

- Frankenstein 2.0, *Roger Morris*
- Facebook Dracula, *Peter Flynn*
- Live Fast, Die Young, *Rupert Morgan*
- Rock Rebels, *Rupert Morgan*

MEET THE CAST

Jack

Debs

Melody

CJ

Jen

Bruno

Professor Strictly
Head teacher

Marguerite

Pete the Painter

Bus

1

SPRING INTO ACTION!

It's another exciting day at Star School... or not!

Jen is watching TV,

Debs is painting her nails.

Melody and Pete are listening to music.

Bruno is on the Internet and CJ and Jack are playing computer games.

Suddenly Marguerite comes in, looking excited. Behind her is Professor Strictly, who looks... *less* enthusiastic.

Marguerite – Everybody come outside! I've got a surprise for you!!

Melody – Ooh a surprise! I love surprises.

Jen – What is it?

CJ – New instruments?

Pete – New equipment?

Debs – New clothes?

Debs – Chocolate?

They all run downstairs to see what's outside...

Jack – It's just an old bus!

Debs – A VERY old bus.

Bruno – What are we supposed to do with THAT?!

Marguerite – It was so cheap! I just *had* to buy it!

Prof – With school money...

Bruno – But why? Why buy an old bus?

Marguerite – It's my BIG NEW IDEA! We're going to repair it...

Melody – What?

Jack – How?

Bruno – **WHY?**

Marguerite – ...and then we're going on tour*!

Melody – OOH... a tour! Cool!

Prof – Um... just a very small tour.

CJ – It will be great! Now, how do we repair the bus?

***on tour:** *en tournée*

Pete – I'm good with machinery, so I'll look at the motor.

Bruno – I'll equip it with all the gadgets: music... Sat-Nav*... maybe TV!

Melody – I have some great ideas for painting it.

Jack – Jen and I can help you with that.

Debs – Let's put in some curtains! It's going to be so cool!

***Sat-Nav:** *GPS*

2

PLANNING THE TOUR

Marguerite – Here is what I'm thinking...

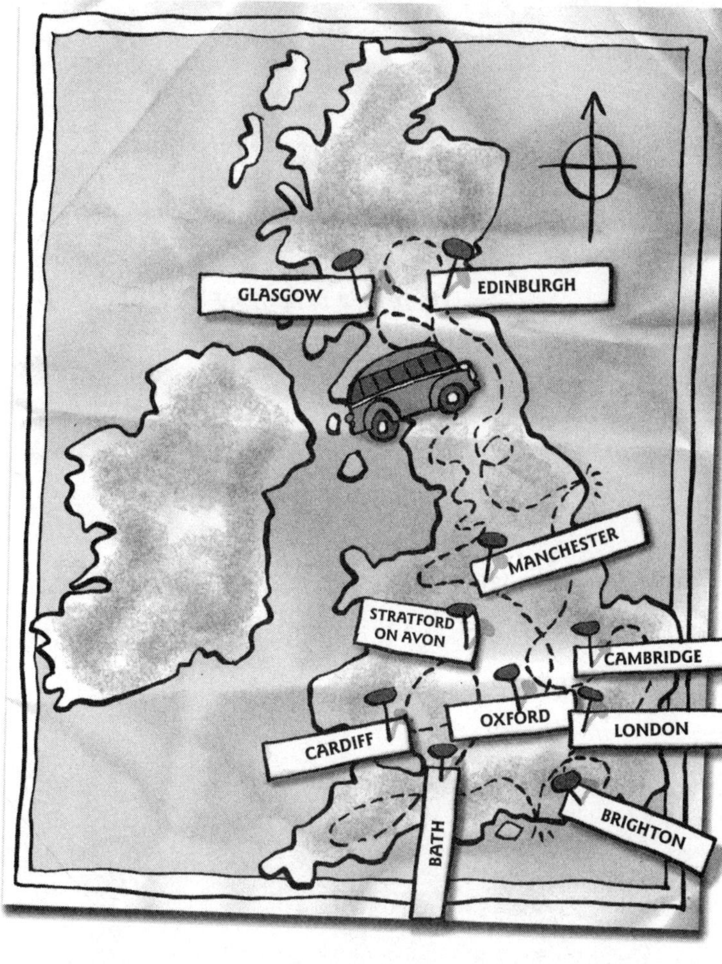

Prof – We can't go to *all* those places, Marguerite!

Melody – Please can we go to Oxford? It's so beautiful!

Jen – We're drama students so we *have* to go to Stratford-upon-Avon. It's William Shakespeare's home town!

CJ – And obviously London is a must!

Jack – But what about–

Prof – **STOP!**

That's enough!

Marguerite – Oh... Professor! Why limit the students' imagination?

Prof – Because we have a limited budget!

Marguerite *(looking disdainful)* – Hmph! As an artiste, I find financial questions *so* vulgar...

3

GOOD AS NEW

For the next month, the Star School students and staff work hard on the old bus.

Finally, it is time to paint the bus.

Melody – I think we want a vintage, hippy look.

Bruno – No way! We need to make the bus look new, shiny, modern.

Pete – We should paint **STAR SCHOOL** on the side and add...

Melody – Stars! We'll add lots of stars!

Debs – Can we make them silver*?

Melody – Whatever colour you want! Everybody join in!

***silver:** *argenté*

By the end of the week, the bus looks like this:

4

PACK IT UP!

Prof Strictly – Time to pack your things, everyone! And remember – we don't have much space in the bus.

But not everyone listens...

Melody – I need my camera... and a sleeping bag... and my books... a tambourine...

CJ – I need my guitar... and my keyboard... my hair gel...

Bruno – Food! We need snacks! Biscuits, cakes, drinks... chocolate... ooh! A roast chicken!

Melody – Sun cream, sunglasses...

Jen – My raincoat... an umbrella...

Debs – I need shoes! My silver ones for the performance. Flip flops in case it's sunny. Boots in case it rains...

Marguerite – A clock, my maps, the radio... a hot water bottle...

Jack – My black jeans... my big coat...

Pete – Stop! Stop! STOP! Look!

They all look at the huge pile of things by the bus.

The Prof – We CAN'T take all this. What are we going to leave behind?

Bruno – Well, we don't need those maps.

Marguerite – A tour with no *maps?* Are you *mad?*

Bruno – But we have the Sat-Nav!

Marguerite – What on earth is that?

Prof – Bruno's right, Marguerite – it is time to move on*!

Marguerite *(looking confused)* – Yes, I know... that's why we need a *map!*

***move on:** 1. *avancer ;* 2. *vivre avec son temps*

5

ON THE ROAD

The Star School bus starts its voyage, guided by Bruno's Sat-Nav:

Sat-Nav: Turn right... turn left, go round the roundabout, after 300 yards take the second left, drive forward for 25 miles... take the exit, turn right...

You have reached your destination
take the exit
drive forward
25
go round the roundabout
300

Marguerite – Stratford-upon-Avon, students! Home of William Shakespeare, the greatest dramatist of all time!

CJ – And now home to... large numbers of photographers?

Jen – They're *tourists,* silly!

CJ – But what is there to see? Shakespeare died 400 years ago! It's boring!

Melody – Well, I think it's a very pretty town.

Bruno – Look... tea shops! We *must* have scones and cream!

Jen – No, I want to visit the Royal Shakespeare Company. I'm going to be a director* there one day!

Bruno – ...and jam?

The students perform outside in the park. The tourists love it.

***director:** *metteur en scène*

Prof Strictly – Well done! That was brilliant!

Debs – Phew! I am *so* tired!

Bruno – Yeah, and hungry! Sir, I think we really need that cream tea now...

Prof Strictly – No time! We have to be in Oxford for tonight's performance! Now... where did we park the bus?

Jack *(imitating the voice of the Sat-Nav)* – Exit the park... cross the road... turn left... continue past the tea shop* ... continue *past* the tea shop, Bruno...

***continue past the tea shop:** *laissez le salon de thé sur votre droite / gauche*

6

OXFORD

The next day the students tour Oxford before they leave for London.

Debs – Wow... I want to study *here!*

Jen – Um... I don't think Oxford is the place for drama students, Debs!

Jack – Yeah, Oxford is for mathematicians.

Melody – And scientists!

Bruno – And politicians – it says here that 25 British Prime Ministers were students at Oxford University!

Melody – So... not the place for dancers, Debs.

Debs – Too bad. I think it's beautiful!

CJ – Ugh! It's just a lot of old buildings! It's not cool like... London!

OXFORD

Prof Strictly – Oh my God! London! We have a performance there tonight! Back to the bus everyone!

Bruno programmes the Sat-Nav for their destination. But, just then, CJ trips and bumps into Melody, who bumps into Jack, and...

Bruno – Ow! You spilled coffee all over me, Jack!

Jack – It wasn't my fault! Melody knocked me!

Melody – It was CJ!

CJ – Hey, don't blame me, guys – it was my **shoes**!

Jack – I'm really sorry, Bruno – are you okay?

Bruno – I'm okay. But I'm not so sure about the Sat-Nav...

7

LOST IN LONDON!

The Star School tour bus arrives in London. But then things start to go wrong...

Sat-Nav – Cross Westminster Bridge... bzzzt!... continue straight...

Marguerite – Where is tonight's performance again, Professor?

Prof – Outside the National Theatre.

Marguerite – That's funny. I think the National Theatre is on the *other* side of the river.

Sat-Nav – Turn left... continue past St. James' Park... bzzt!... you have arrived at your destination.

Melody – Umm... isn't this Buckingham Palace, guys?

Bruno – Oops! I'd better reprogramme the Sat-Nav...

They continue their journey.

Sat-Nav – Take the next left... continue straight for one mile... turn left again... *bzzt!*... continue straight... take the next left... continue straight for one mile... turn left...

Jack – Guys, are we going in a circle?

Bruno – Sorry! I'll fix* it!

***fix:** *réparer*

They continue searching for the National Theatre, but the Sat-Nav has its own ideas.

Sat-Nav – ...Turn right... continue straight... you have arrived at your destination!

CJ – Personally, Jack, I don't think this is the National Theatre.

Jack – Bruno – why does your Sat-Nav think there is a theatre in the Tower of London?

Marguerite – Hmph! *"Don't be silly, Marguerite. We have a Sat-Nav, Marguerite..."*

8

ON THE WRONG SIDE OF TOWN...

As darkness falls, the Star School bus is more and more lost...

Melody – We are *so* not at the National Theatre, guys...

Prof Strictly – I *knew* this tour was a bad idea!

Jack – Looks like there's no London performance for us.

Bruno – And I'm hungry...

Marguerite – Yes, but do you want to know what the *real* problem is?

All – *What?*

Marguerite – We're out of petrol.

Melody – Uh-oh...

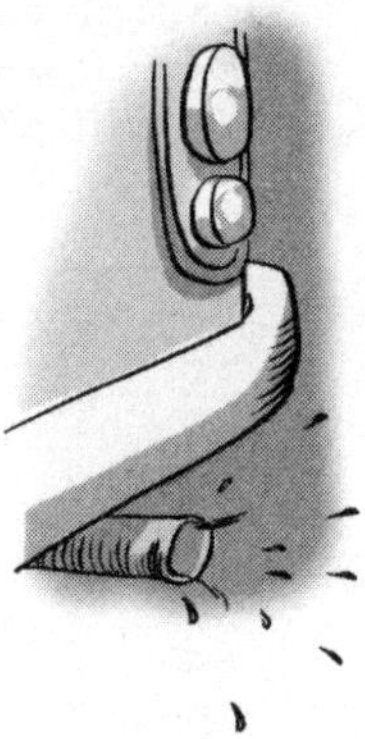

The bus stops beside an old industrial building. They get out to look around. They see an abandoned cinema, some closed up shops, and houses with broken windows.

All is dark and silent. Except... there is light coming from inside the old industrial building. And voices... *shouts and screams.*

Prof Strictly – Errrr... perhaps we should go back to the bus!

Jen – I can hear footsteps*. Someone's coming.

LET'S RUN! RUN! RUN!

Debs – In these shoes? I won't get far. Stay with me everyone. Don't leave me!

The door slides open...

A man steps forward into the streetlight...

***footsteps:** *bruits de pas*

Man – Star School? Are you here to perform?

Prof – Perform? Yes... I mean, no... that is... perform what?

Man – This is a poetry slam, man!

Prof – Sorry? A poetry *what?*

CJ – Don't you know what a poetry slam is? This is so cool, guys – we can do this!

All – Do what?

CJ – It's a competition. Come on – we *are* going to perform in London tonight, after all!

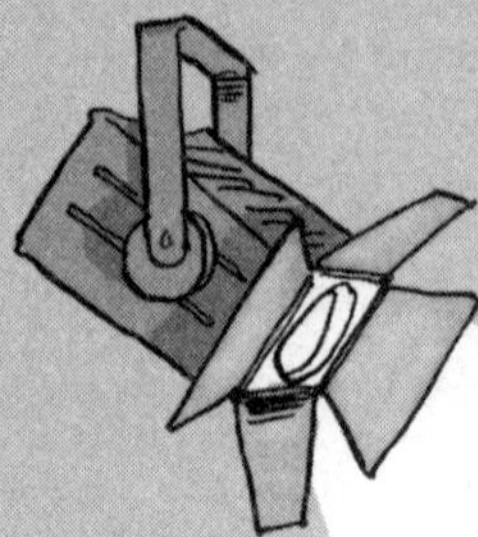

9

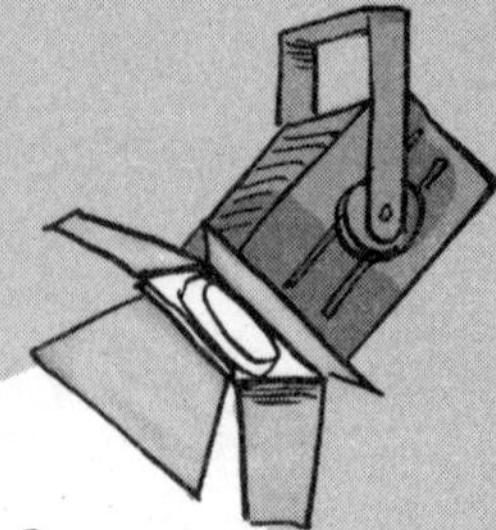

THE SLAM!

Inside the building, the students find themselves on a stage. The lights come up. A large, noisy crowd is waiting for them to perform...

CJ – It's okay, guys. Just do what I do!

He steps forward to the microphone.

CJ – It's a Poetry Slam! Poetry Slam!
Listen up I'll tell you who I am!
I'm CJ! Yeah, CJ's my name
Poetry and rap – that's my game!
Meet Jack – he's so great...

Jack – Er... even if I got here late!

Melody – I'm Melody – here's Bruno, Deb, Jen and Pete...

Marguerite – Don't forget me! I'm Marguerite.

Send your voice to the back of the room
You can make it loud Boom BOOM BOOM!

CJ – So now you know who I am

I'll show you all how to slam!

Stand up tall,

Stand up proud!

Jack – You can speak *softly!*

Bruno – Or say it **loud!**

Melody – Stand still and strong,

Don't be shy!

Debs – Just find the words and
Let them fly!

CJ – And when it's over,
What do you do now?
Face the audience and...

TAKE A BOW!

The audience clap and cheer and shout and scream. When the votes are counted, the Star School students are...

in bottom position*.

CJ – Ooops! Oh well... at least it was fun.

Melody – I loved it! I want to do it again!

Jack – Yeah, can we come back?

Prof – No! No more tours!

Marguerite – Oh... very well.

Prof – You agree? You're not going to argue?

Marguerite – No.

Prof – Well... that was easier than I expected.

Marguerite – Listen, everybody! We're having a Poetry Slam at Star School next month... and **you're all invited!**

Star School students – Yesss! Brilliant!

The audience all applaud as Marguerite leaves the stage.

***in bottom position:** *à la dernière place*

Prof – Marguerite… what… what… what have you done?

Marguerite – It's my **BIG NEW IDEA!**

paper planes teens

C'est aussi un site :

www.paperplanesteens.fr

• Plonge-toi dans l'histoire
en écoutant la **version audio** !

• Retrouve **toutes les infos** sur l'actualité
de la collection (auteurs, illustrateurs,
nouveautés, événements...)